P9-CFF-354

THE MAGICIAN'S HAT

Written by MALCOLM MITCHELL

Illustrated by JOANNE LEW-VRIETHOFF

ORCHARD BOOKS
An Imprint of Scholastic Inc.

Library of Congress Cataloging-in-Publication Data available

ISBN 978-1-338-11454-6

10 9 8 7 6 5 4 3 2 1   18 19 20 21 22

Printed in China   62
First edition, March 2018

The text type was set in Skippy Sharp.
The display type was set in Baboon Regular.
Book design by Christine Kettner

To my mother, for always allowing
me to believe dreams can become reality.
—M.M.

For Mom and Dad. You are my Magic.
And for Andrea P. and Mela B.,
greatest Magicians for making all things possible.
—J.L.-V.

Family Fun Day at the library was filled with exciting events.

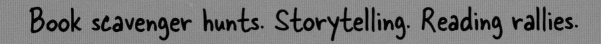

Book scavenger hunts. Storytelling. Reading rallies.

Today, for the first time, a magician arrived with a bag of tricks and a BIG hat. Everyone gathered around to see the Magician perform.

He bent a spoon, just by looking at it.

He made
playing cards
float in front
of his nose.

The Magician could even make a coin appear from a puppy's ear.

When he waved his wand, a banana vanished.

This was just the warm-up act. Now the Magician was ready to DAZZLE the crowd with his favorite trick of all. The Magician's magic started with a story.

"When I was a kid, my mom and dad brought me to this library on Family Fun Day. During the book scavenger hunt, I wandered into the reading room."

"There were hundreds of books.
Books about dogs.
Books about planes.
Books about the sun, flowers, rain,
cities, and circus dancers.

Out of the hundreds of books,
one special book jumped out at me.
It was a book about
MAGIC!"

"I read and read and read. Every single word, on every single page. I discovered that book wasn't just about MAGIC. I learned that books are magic. Even though I was still in the library, those pages and words took me places I had always DREAMED of going.

The Family Fun Day crowd had grown. Kids from all over town were eager to see more of the Magician's magic. He asked them, "What do *you* want to be when *you* grow up?"

Amy shouted, "I want to be a dentist!"

The Magician invited Amy to reach inside his hat.
Amy dug deep, then deeper, until she felt something . . .

"It's . . . it's . . . a BOOK!" Amy shouted.
The Magician asked, "What is your
book about?"

"My book's about teeth.
Cleaning teeth.
And fixing teeth.
And X-rays."

Right away, like MAGIC, Amy saw herself holding dental tools, a toothbrush, and a rinsing cup. But in the library, where everyone could see, Amy was hugging her book and smiling.

Matt had been watching closely. After seeing Amy's magic, he wondered, *What else is in that hat?* He called out, "I want to be a famous football player!"

And so, the Magician offered Matt his hat. "Let's see what magic you can find inside."

Matt reached in. Way down, there was something that couldn't fit into just one hand. Matt plunged both hands into the hat, and *pulled*.

"It's a book about football. It even . . . has . . . my name on it!"

All at once, like MAGIC, Matt was on the field.

Ryan called out from the back of the crowd. "Wait a second! This is not magic! Amy's and Matt's parents must have told the Magician what they want to be when they grow up."

The Magician asked Ryan, "What do you want to be when you grow up?"

This was Ryan's chance to prove that the Magician was a fake. He snickered and said, "A dog!"

The Magician asked Ryan to reach into his magical hat.

Ryan said, "I can't feel anything."

"Sometimes you must really reach and stretch for what you want to be. That's part of the MAGIC."

Ryan reached deeper and deeper until his fingers grabbed on to something.

He clutched a BEAUTIFUL BOOK that had nothing to do with dogs.

Its pages were filled with letters, and paintings, and photos, and foldouts.

STARS.

PLANETS.

ROCKET SHIPS.

Ryan had always DREAMED of becoming an astronaut and exploring the wide-open sky, hurtling into outer space, and zooming to a far-off galaxy.

"Whoa," whispered Ryan. "How did you do that?"

"I am not doing anything," the Magician said. "You are."

"I am?" asked Ryan. "But there's got to be a secret trick in those books."

"The desires that are within you bring out the magic in these books. Follow your DREAMS and they will take you wherever you want to go."

"What are your dreams?"

The Magician turned his hat so everyone could see inside.